## MAKE 5 WISHES

### VOLUME 1

Starring Avril Lavigne
Concept by Camilla d'Errico
Story by Camilla d'Errico
and Joshua Dysart
Script by Joshua Dysart
Art by Camilla

BALLANTINE BOOKS • NEW YORK

D1509606

A Del Rey Trade Paperback Original

Published in the United States by Del Rey Books, an imprint of The Random House Publishing Group, a division of Random House, Inc., New York.

DEL REY is a registered trademark and the Del Rey colophon is a trademark of Random House, Inc.

Some of the artwork contained in this work is preexisting.

ISBN 978-0-345-50058-8

Printed in the United States of America

www.delreybooks.com

9 8 7 6 5 4 3 2

Project direction by House of Parlance Media, www.houseofparlance.com
Coloring: Dave McCaig
Background Art and Additional Coloring: Sunder Raj
Lettering: Ed Brisson
Cover Art: Camilla d'Errico
Cover Design: Dreu Pennington-McNeil

# CONTENTS

I'LL START WITH THE RAIN.

'CAUSE RAIN IS SOMETHING THAT'S CLEAR AND REAL...

AND MY STORY IS HARD ENOUGH *TO BELIEVE AS IT IS.*

ALSO... THE RAIN OBSCURES WITHOUT LYING...

AND I DON'T KNOW WHICH PARTS OF MY STORY ARE REAL ANYMORE...

# A MESSAGE FROM AVRIL

I love writing and performing music. I enjoy acting and I'm excited at the opportunity to create a graphic novel.

Camilla d'Errico showed me her early sketches of Hana and the demon who comes into her life, and I was excited to find out more about Hana, who she is and what would happen to her.

Joshua Dysart and I worked closely with Camilla to come up with a story that we think you'll like. What if you were given five wishes? What would they be?

I really want to know what you think of Make 5 Wishes. Please let me know by leaving a message at www.make5wishes.com.

Love,

MY NAME IS HANA...

AND WHICH PARTS ARE PHANTOMS OF MY MEMORY.

UP UNTIL VERY RECENTLY I USED TO FEEL LIKE THIS FLY I ONCE SAW IN CLASS.

BANGING ITS HEAD AGAINST THE INVISIBLE *BARRIER* OVER AND OVER AGAIN.

BUZZING AWAY. DESPERATE TO ESCAPE INTO A LARGER WORLD.

SO HUNGRY FOR SOMETHING NEW... AND NO ONE EVEN NOTICING.

I *WAS* SMALL, TOO. INVISIBLE.

GOT IT!!

UGH!

NO. NOT INVISIBLE. BEING INVISIBLE WOULD'VE BEEN COOL.

I JUST WASN'T *WORTH NOTICING.*

IN CONCERT

avril lavigne

I CAN'T BELIEVE WE'RE DOING THIS! YOU JUST GOT HOME AND WE'RE ALREADY FIGHTING!

BECAUSE YOU WON'T GET OFF MY BACK!! YOU WANT ME TO BE AT HOME MORE, BUT I'M WORKING ALL THE TIME...

AVRIL LAVIGNE!!

COME ON, HANA!!

LOOK, I WASN'T CRAZY. I NEVER THOUGHT SHE WAS REALLY THERE OR ANYTHING.

BUT HER MUSIC ALWAYS WAS.

IT WAS IN EVERY PART OF MY LIFE. AND EVEN THOUGH IT SEEMED TO COME FROM SO FAR AWAY...

IT STILL FELT LIKE IT WAS AIMED RIGHT AT ME...

LIKE A MISSILE!!

HER MUSIC TOOK AWAY THE NUMBNESS.

HONEY!!

WE CAN HEAR YOU DOWN-STAIRS!

DAD AND I ARE TRYING TO...

TRYING TO HAVE A TALK! PLEASE!

AND MADE ME FEEL LESS ALONE.

THE NEXT DAY.

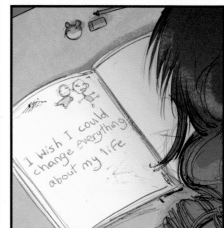

I wish I could change everything about my life

OKAY, EVERYONE, I'VE GRADED YOUR SHORT STORIES.

NEXT WEEK WE GO OVER THESE ALOUD IN CLASS.

MR. TERRY, MY LIT TEACHER, ONCE READ US THIS POEM THAT SAID PEOPLE WERE LIKE OCEANS.

GOOD, BRIAN,

VERY IMAGINATIVE.

A LOT OF THE KIDS DIDN'T REALLY GET WHAT THAT MEANT. BUT I THINK I UNDERSTOOD.

AND PAR FOR THE COURSE,

I REMEMBER, AT THE TIME, WISHING I COULD WRITE THAT GOOD.

WE GET NOTHING FROM... UH... HANA.

THAT'S ANOTHER F, HANA.

*God what an idiot.*

*Shut up, I think she's slow or something.*

I FOUND MR. TERRY ON A LOCAL FREE DATING SITE AND ANSWERED HIS AD.

I SENT A PICTURE OF MY AUNT, AND TOLD HIM I LOVED TO READ THE CLASSICS.

THE PICTURE HE SENT BACK OF HIMSELF WAS FROM, LIKE, 10 YEARS AGO OR SOMETHING.

IN MY FIRST E-MAIL I TOLD HIM I WAS READING MOBY-DICK.

THAT E-MAIL WAS TWO SENTENCES LONG.

HE SENT ME BACK A THREE-PAGE ESSAY ABOUT THE BOOK.

I DIDN'T HAVE TO WRITE SMART THINGS TO HIM. HE WANTED ME, OR HER, TO BE SMART.

SO HE JUST ASSUMED I WAS.

MOBY-DICK

LONELY PEOPLE ARE THE EASIEST TO FOOL.

SO WHAT ABOUT BRIAN?

HE'S CUTE.

I GUESS, IN A DORKY SORT OF WAY.

ROSE I FOUND ON A HIP-HOP CULTURE BLOG, BUT IT TOOK SOME DIGGING ON SEARCH ENGINES.

SHE CALLED HERSELF DJ PLASTIC TAGS.

HER PROFILE SAID SHE WAS A 25-YEAR-OLD BRAZILIAN GIRL.

SO, UHM... ROSE...

WHAT WAS YOUR STORY FOR MR. TERRY'S CLASS ABOUT?

WE E-MAILED EACH OTHER ALL THE TIME TO TALK ABOUT MUSIC.

SHE THOUGHT I WAS SOMEONE OLDER, TOO.

I THINK JACK IS CUTE.

I DIG THAT PUNK THING HE'S GOT GOING ON.

GROSS!

HE'S LIKE 16! HE'S TOO OLD!

THEN THERE WAS JESSICA.

I FOUND JESSICA IN A RELIGIOUS CHAT ROOM AFTER SEEING HER PRAY BEFORE EATING LUNCH ONE DAY.

SHE THINKS I'M AN OLDER MAN WITH LOTS OF MONEY WHO'S LOST FAITH IN GOD AND IS CONTEMPLATING SUICIDE.

NOT UNTIL IT WAS TOO LATE.

OF COURSE I HUNG OUT MOSTLY ON THE AVRIL BOARDS.

I WAS ALL KINDS OF PEOPLE THERE.

A MUSICIAN LOOKING FOR WORK. A FAMOUS ACTRESS WHO WANTED TO DO A MOVIE WITH AVRIL.

A FAN WITH TERMINAL CANCER.

AVRIL LAVIGNE

THERE WAS SOMETHING ABOUT THAT WEBSITE.

SOMETHING HIDDEN BETWEEN THE LINES OF CODE OR...

I CAN'T EXPLAIN IT.

WHATCHA DOIN'?

UHM, JUST...

JUST LOOKING AT THIS WEBSITE.

MAKE5WISHES.COM? OH GOD, YOU'RE NOT FALLING FOR SOME INTERNET SCAM, ARE YOU?

NO!

I'M NOT STUPID!

THE MUSIC'S BEEN OVER FOR AN HOUR, HANA.

I COULDN'T STOP STARING AT IT. IT MADE ME FEEL SO STRANGE... LIKE, FUZZY SOMEHOW.

HANA, YOU'RE STILL UP?

IT TOOK THE SOUND OF MY MOTHER KNOCKING ON MY DOOR TO PULL ME AWAY.

HANA, SAY SOMETHING.

LOOK, BABY, I WANT TO GET YOU AWAY FROM THIS ROOM...

I WANT YOU TO LEARN HOW TO SPEND TIME WITH PEOPLE, YOU KNOW? SO I FOUND THIS PROGRAM...

IT PLACES CHILDREN WITH THE ELDERLY WHO HAVE NO ONE TO SPEND TIME WITH.

AND I'VE FOUND THIS REALL SWEET, INTERESTIN OLD MAN AND HE' DYING TO BE AROUND A YOUNG PERSON.

I THINK THIS WILL REALLY HELP YOU...

HELP YOU COME OUT OF YOUR SHELL.

HI, HANA.

HONEY, WHEN'S THE LAST TIME WE TALKED?

HAVE WE EVER?

UHM... HI, DAD.

IS IT THAT YOU HATE ME?

HMMM... I JUST... UH...

YES? SAY IT. SAY WHAT'S ON YOUR MIND.

JUST DOESN'T SEEM LIKE THERE'S MUCH WORTH SAYING, I GUESS.

OF COURSE THERE'RE THINGS WORTH SAYING, LIKE, "I LOVE YOU."

I LOVE YOU, HANA.

I USED TO THINK YOU WERE JUST REALLY SHY,

BUT IT'S SOMETHING ELSE, ISN'T IT?

SHE'S AFRAID. AFRAID OF LIFE.

WHAT DID YOU SAY TO ME?

Shut up.

NO, NOTHING NOT YOU

LOOK, IF I'VE DONE SOMETHING TO PUSH YOU AWAY, JUST TELL ME.

YOU CAN YELL AT ME IF YOU NEED TO.

AT LEAST AN ARGUMENT WOULD BE SOME KIND OF COMMUNICATIO—

HANA, WAIT!

PLEASE!

THAT SATURDAY WAS MY FIRST DAY AS A RENTED GRANDCHILD.

HELLO, MR. WESTON! GOOD TO SEE YOU AGAIN!

HE WAS GROSS.

HIS SPOTTED SKIN LOOKED LIKED IT WAS TRYING TO SLIDE OFF HIS BONES.

OH, GOOD, GOOD. HELLO!

AND HE SMELLED LIKE ROTTEN LAUNDRY.

YOU MUST BE HANA.

YOUR GARDEN IS SO LOVELY.

OH, THANK YOU, YES... I, WELL... IT WAS MY WIFE'S.

WHEN SHE DIED I LEARNED HOW TO KEEP IT UP.

IT'S GOOD FOR THE MIND TO LEARN NEW THINGS LATE IN LIFE, YOU KNOW.

IT WAS DARK AND MUSTY IN HIS HOUSE.

WE SAT IN SILENCE FOR A LONG TIME BEFORE EITHER OF US SPOKE.

HMM...

WELL, I MUST ADMIT THIS IS A LITTLE STRANGE. ISN'T IT?

SOMEWHERE, I DON'T KNOW WHERE, WAS THIS TICKING CLOCK...

AND EVEN THAT SOUNDED OLD, SLOW, CREAKY.

IT'S BEEN A LONG TIME SINCE I HAD A YOUNG PERSON IN THE HOUSE.

THERE'S NOT REALLY MUCH TO DO AROUND HERE.

DO YOU HAVE E-MAIL?

NO, NO COMPUTER.

OH, I KNOW! DO YOU LIKE MUSIC, HANA?

I WAS A FINE JAZZ GUITARIST IN MY DAY.

THE ARTHRITIS KEEPS ME FROM PLAYING NOW, BUT I USED TO REALLY SWING.

YOU KNOW WHAT A RECORD IS?

OH GOD...

OH... OF COURSE YOU DO...

SORRY...

I JUST DIDN'T KNOW WITH ALL THE UHM... M3 PLAYERS TODAY.

RIGHT, WELL, THIS IS MY OLD BAND.

LISTEN.

YOU LIKE IT?

DON'T SAY WHAT YOU'RE THINKING.

HE'S TRYING TO BE NICE.

STOP IT, HANA.

IT'S SLOW...

IT'S BORING.

MY MOTHER JUST DROPPED ME OFF SO I'D BE OUT OF HER HAIR WHILE SHE TRIES TO MAKE MY DAD LOVE HER AGAIN.

THIS IS STUPID. I DON'T WANT TO BE HERE.

SO I'M STUCK HANGING OUT WITH SOME OLD FART WHO'S JUST WAITING AROUND TO DIE!

I WANT TO GO HOME!!

HANA, JUST STOP TALKING FOR A SECOND AND THINK ABOUT WHAT YOU'RE SAYING.

I SEE. OF COURSE YOU DON'T WANT TO BE HERE.

WHY WOULD YOU?

AND AT THAT MOMENT IT HAD ALL BECOME TOO MUCH.

I WAS SICK OF IT.

SICK OF SCHOOL, SICK OF MY PARENTS, SICK OF MY BEST FRIEND NOT EVEN BEING REAL.

SICK OF IT ALL.

MAKE5WISHES

Order Now!

AND I WAS WILLING TO DO WHATEVER I HAD TO DO TO CHANGE IT.

MY FIRST DAY AS A
RENTED GRANDCHILD HAD
BEEN A DISASTER.

I HADN'T WANTED
TO BE THERE AND
I MADE IT CLEAR.

NOT THIS AGAIN.

DON'T GET SUCKERED IN, HANA. YOU'RE SMARTER THAN THIS.

Order Now

I DIDN'T FEEL DUMB ABOUT FALLING FOR THE WEBSITE AT ALL.

THE BIZARRE SENSATION I FELT THAT FIRST NIGHT WHEN I FOUND THE SITE...

WAS GROWING INSIDE OF ME.

I COULD FEEL THE BOX GETTING CLOSER.

IT WASN'T A BAD FEELING...

IT WASN'T A GOOD FEELING.

JUST A, UHM... A PRESENCE...

I GUESS.

I WAS
PRACTICALLY
BUZZING.

THERE WAS
SOMETHING INSIDE.
A WEIGHT SHIFTING
AROUND.

MAYBE IT WAS BECAUSE OF THAT STRANGE FEELING THE WEBSITE HAD GIVEN ME...

BUT I JUST KNEW WHATEVER WAS INSIDE THAT BOX WOULD CHANGE MY LIFE FOREVER.

I'M GLAD YOU'RE NOT SCARED OF ME, HANA.

YOU'RE SCARED OF FAR TOO MANY THINGS, AS IT IS.

WHO ARE YOU?

ME? I'M A SUPER-DUPER MENDER OF LONELY HEARTS, SUNSHINE!

I'M A DOZEN POP SONGS ABOUT LOVE ALL ROLLED INTO ONE!

I DANCE A MEAN CHA-CHA AND COOK A TIRAMISÙ TO DIE FOR.

I'M AN ANGEL TO DEMONS...

AND A DEMON TO ANGELS.

HE'S CUTE. I MEAN, YEAH HE'S FREAKY... BUT I'M FREAKY, YOU KNOW. AND BESIDES...

IT'S SOMETHING REAL. SOMETHING I CAN TOUCH.

SHHH... RICHARD, STOP YELLING. HANA'S IN THE KITCHEN. I HEAR HER TALKING TO HERSELF AGAIN.

BUSTED.

SO WHAT'RE YOU GONNA WISH FOR?

EVERYTHING!

SO, ABOUT THESE WISHES?

ON TO THE MEAT OF THE MATTER!

UHM... YEAH... YOU SAID SOMETHING ABOUT... LEGAL SOMETHING?

LEGALESE, MA PETITE SPARROW!

THE SMALL PRINT BEAR TRAPS AT THE BOTTOM OF THE PACKAGING!

HUH.

THOSE WHO LONG KNOW NOT WHERE CONTENTMENT LIES TREAD GENTLY T... REALM OF DREAM...

I'LL JUST BE TURNING IN THEN,

LONG TRIP AND ALL.

GOOD NIGHT, AVRIL.

AND SO LIFE WITH MY FUNNY LITTLE WALKING, TALKING DOLL BEGAN.

RIGHT OUT OF THE BOX HE WAS MY FRIEND. HE NEVER JUDGED ME. HE NEVER IGNORED ME.

AND NOT ONCE DID IT OCCUR TO HIM THAT I WAS WEIRD. BECAUSE LET'S FACE IT...

HE WAS THE WEIRDEST OF ALL.

AND HE WANTED TO DO EVERYTHING I WANTED TO DO!

WE DANCED BEHIND THE TRACKS WHILE WAITING FOR THE RED LINE TO TAKE US TO SCHOOL.

WE HUNG OUR HEADS OUT THE TRAIN WINDOW UNTIL WATER POURED FROM OUR EYES.

WE PEED OUTSIDE!

(I ALWAYS WANTED TO PEE OUTSIDE.)

IT WAS ALL SO AMAZING!

I WAS ALMOST NERVOUS TO START ASKING FOR WISHES.

WORRIED THAT WHEN THEY WERE ALL GONE MY FRIEND WOULD GO AWAY TOO.

BUT WOULD I EVEN NEED HIM THEN?

ONCE MOM AND DAD FELL IN LOVE AGAIN.

ONCE I DIDN'T HAVE TO DEAL WITH MR. WESTON ANYMORE.

ONCE BRIAN HAD NOTICED ME FOR MY CREATIVITY AND INNER BEAUTY...

OKAY... I THINK I'M READY FOR MY FIRST WISH.

I WANT TO DO A TEST WISH FIRST...

SOMETHING HARMLESS, JUST TO SEE HOW IT ALL WORKS, YOU KNOW?

THAT'S COOL, BUT YOU ONLY GET FIVE WISHES, HANA.

FOUR WILL BE PLENTY TO ASK FOR WORLD PEACE. SO UHM...HOW DOES IT WORK?

SPEAK YOUR DESIRE AS PLAINLY AS POSSIBLE, THEN BREAK OFF ONE OF MY HORNS.

REALLY? THAT'S WEIRD.

YEAH, IT'S KIND OF GROSS AND GROWING THEM BACK SUCKS. I DIDN'T MAKE THE RULES.

OKAY... HERE WE GO...

I WANT BRIAN TO NOTICE ME.

AHH, BRIAN, GOLDEN APPLE OF THE SCHOOL HALLS. FINE, THEN, SO LET'S DO THIS!

HEY, WHAT'S YOUR PROBLEM, JESSICA? SHE'S NOT A RETARD.

You're not a retard, are you?

UHM...

NO!

NO.

WELL, THAT'S WHAT ROSE TOLD ME, ANYWAY.

I DID NOT!

SHE'S NEVER DONE ANYTHING TO YOU. JUST BACK OFF, OKAY? SHE HURT HERSELF.

FORGET THEM, THEY'RE IDIOTS. I'LL SEE YOU AROUND... AT LUNCH MAYBE.

YEAH, OKAY.

BUT WHEN THE HEART OF A CHILD SKIPS A BEAT...

YOU'RE INSIDE OF HIM NOW.

IT'S LIKE AN EARTHQUAKE HAS STRUCK THEM.

OH MY GOD!

THAT WAS AWESOME!! HE TOTALLY LOOKED RIGHT INTO MY EYES!

NO, HANA. HE DIDN'T JUST LOOK AT YOU.

HE SAW YOU. REALLY SAW YOU FOR THE FIRST TIME.

YOU MADE HIS HEART SKIP A BEAT.

WHEN AN ADULT LOOKS AT BEAUTY AND THEIR HEART SKIPS, IT'S AS COMMON AS A SIGH.

WOW, YOU SAY COOL STUFF SOMETIMES.

COURSE I DO,

I'M A FORCE OF MAGIC IN A DIME-STORE WORLD! YOU WANT ME TO TALK LIKE A BUM?

SO... DO YOU THINK YOU COULD MAKE THE WHOLE SCHOOL NOTICE ME LIKE THAT?

IN A GOOD WAY, I MEAN. HAVE THEM ALL TREAT ME LIKE I WAS SOMETHING SPECIAL.

WELL, YEAH— BUT IT WOULD COST ANOTHER WISH.

THAT STILL LEAVES ME THREE. THAT'S PLENTY OF WISHES FOR WORLD PEACE AND STUFF.

IF YOU'RE SURE, HANA. LIKE I SAID, I DON'T MAKE THE RULES—

FIVE HORNS IS ALL I HAVE TO GIVE.

SO IT GOES.

C'MON, HANA. LET'S ROLL!

I COULDN'T WAIT TO SEE WHAT MY NEW FRIEND HAD IN STORE FOR ME AT SCHOOL.

FALLING INTO BRIAN'S ARMS HAD BEEN SO AMAZING.

FOR THAT SHORT SPACE OF TIME, HE TREATED ME AS IF I WAS SOMEONE VALUABLE TO HIM.

WHAT WOULD IT FEEL LIKE WHEN THE WHOLE SCHOOL TREATED ME LIKE THAT?

UNLIKE ANYTHING I'D EVER FELT BEFORE.

AND I WAS DESPERATE TO KEEP THAT MOMENT CLOSE AND REAL, TO NOT LET THE SENSATION FADE.

UNFORTUNATELY, IT WAS ONLY FRIDAY NIGHT.

MEANING I'D HAVE TO WAIT FOREVER...

ALL WEEKEND, JUST TO SEE HOW THINGS WOULD TURN OUT.

Dear Mr. Terry,

I'm so sorry for the delay in writing you back. I've been alone for a long time, and, admittedly there's some fear now in approaching you.

But your e-mail was so thoughtful and intelligent that I finally caved in.

THAT NIGHT I HAD A DREAM.

THEN I SAW AVRIL.

I HADN'T THOUGHT ABOUT HER MUCH SINCE MY NEW FRIEND ARRIVED.

I CALLED OUT, BUT SHE COULDN'T HEAR ME.

I TRIED TO SWIM TO HER...

BUT A CURRENT KEPT ME FROM MOVING FORWARD.

IN MY MIND I HEARD HER VOICE.

"SOMETHING'S WRONG," SHE SAID.

"SOMETHING'S WRONG."

AND THEN IT HAPPENED.

NNH!

WAIT! WAIT! THINK THIS THROUGH, SWEET CHILD O' MINE. NO MPASSIONED WISHES.

BESIDES, I COULDN'T GET YOU OUT OF TODAY EVEN IF I WANTED TO. FEW WISHES ARE INSTANTANEOUS.

EVEN WITH MY MAGIC TO HELP 'EM ALONG.

FINE, WHATEVER. JUST DO IT!

AND THAT WAS IT. I ONLY HAD TWO WISHES LEFT.

AH, HANA. I WAS AFRAID I MIGHT NOT SEE YOU AGAIN.

NO, MR. WESTON. HANA HAS A LOT TO LEARN ABOUT BEING NICE TO PEOPLE.

I JUST HOPE YOU DON'T HAVE ANY HARD FEELINGS ABOUT LAST WEEK.

YOU...YOU WANT TO APOLOGIZE TO ME?

HANA, I WANTED TO APOLOGIZE FOR Y BEHAVIOR DURING OUR LAST VISIT.

I DID THIS PROGRAM SO THAT I COULD BE AROUND A YOUNG PERSON.

WAS FEELING LESS ND LESS ALIVE, SO OUT OF STEP WITH EVERYTHING.

PEOPLE ARE WALKING AROUND WITH PHONES IN THEIR EARS. TOURISTS ARE GOING UP INTO OUTER SPACE.

AND LIFE, IT HAS THIS WAY OF SQUEEZING PASSION FROM YOU.

I WAS JUST AFRAID OF LOSING MYSELF, OF NO LONGER BEING INSPIRED BY THINGS.

AREN'T YOU EVER AFRAID OF ANYTHING, HANA?

HMM... YES. WELL, ANYWAY, I BROUGHT YOU HERE TO MAKE ME FEEL YOUNG AGAIN.

A SELFISH THING TO DO, I GUESS.

BUT THEN THE FIRST THING I DID WAS ACT OLD AND RIGID AND UNIMAGINATIVE.

HE APOLOGIZED TO ME. I WAS THE ONE WHO WAS MEAN, BUT HE WAS THE ONE WHO WAS SORRY.

FORGIVE ME. I PROMISE TO BE MORE OPEN FROM NOW ON. OKAY?

UM... I... SHOULDN'T HAVE SAID THOSE THINGS THE OTHER DAY. I KNEW BETTER.

WAS IT MY LITTLE WISHING FRIEND WHO HAD GIVEN ME THIS NEWFOUND, UM...

WHAT'S IT CALLED? EMPATHY, I GUESS.

OR WAS IT ME, ALL ON MY OWN?

I COULDN'T SAY.

ALL I KNEW WAS THAT I HAD A SUDDEN OVERWHELMING URGE TO HUG HIM.

OH HANA, WHAT A SWEET GIRL YOU ARE.

I'M SO SORRY WE GOT OFF ON THE WRONG FOOT.

HANCOCK PARK

MOBY-DIC

YOU LOOK GOOD.

DID YOU HAVE A FUN VISIT WITH MR. WESTON?

YEAH.

IT'S NICE TO SEE YOU HAPPY, HANA.

UHM... DO YOU THINK I COULD TAKE BACK A WISH?

I'VE CHANGED MY MIND ABOUT MR. WESTON. I LIKE HIM. HE'S NICE.

OH, HANA, I'M SORRY.

YOU'VE BROKEN THE HORN. IT'S OUT OF MY HANDS.

WHAT DO YOU MEAN?

I'M NOT THE ONE WHO CONTROLS THESE THINGS. YOU'VE SENT YOUR DESIRE OUT INTO THE FOUR CORNERS OF THE WORLD.

THE WISHING ENGINE IS ALREADY CHURNING.

WHYYYYY!

WHY ARE YOU DOING THIS TO US, RICHARD!?

ONE FUNNY THING ABOUT WISHES IS HOW JUST CASTING ONE COULD MAKE ME FEEL BETTER.

I THINK THAT'S HOW I FELT THAT NIGHT AFTER SEEING MY MOM AND DAD HAVE THEIR WORST FIGHT EVER.

AND SO, JUST LIKE THAT, I WAS COMMITTED TO MAKING MY FOURTH WISH.

EVEN THOUGH I'D MADE THREE ALREADY AND ONLY ONE HAD COME TRUE SO FAR.

I WANT MOM AND DAD TO BE HAPPY.

THAT'S AN EASY ONE, SUGAR PLUM!

I HAD ONE WISH LEFT. BUT I WANTED TO SIT ON IT.

TO THINK ABOUT IT.

SEE HOW THE OTHERS TURNED OUT.

Dear Jessica,

We are saddened to inform you…

that the gentleman you have been in communication with at this e-mail address…

has passed away due to a self-inflicted gunshot wound.

Dear Brian,

I don't know if I've mentioned this before... but my dad works for a video game company and he's asked me for some ideas.

I thought of you and how creative and cool you are.

If you want to start working on a pitch of some kind I'll show it to my dad as soon as you're done.

Thanx for the help!

♪ CLICKITY CLICK! CLACK! CLACK! ♫

♪ DON'T ♪ TALK BACK!! ♪

Dear DJ Plastic Tags,

I'm freelancing for a hip-hop magazine in the States right now and they need some write-ups!

Do you think you could find some undiscovered groups in your area and do an article for us?

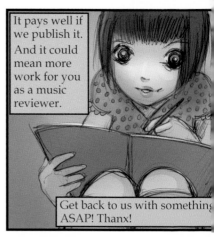

It pays well if we publish it. And it could mean more work for you as a music reviewer.

Get back to us with something ASAP! Thanx!

MR. WESTON'S GARDEN.

HHHHOOONEYY...

AHHH!

Oh... God...
Oh, God...

I THINK I'LL GO SEE MR. WESTON TODAY.

AHH, HONEY... I DON'T THINK THAT'S SUCH A WISE IDEA.

GOING AGAINST THE GRAIN OF A WISH IS A HARD WAY TO TRAVEL, YOU DIG?

I CAN SEE HIM IF I WANT TO!

YES, YES, YOU CAN.

OUR DAUGHTER'S GOING OUTSIDE TO WORK IN A GARDEN.

I TOLD YOU SHE WAS TURNING AROUND.

MR. WESTON?

MR. WESTON! I KNOW WE DIDN'T HAVE A, LIKE AN APPOINTMENT OR ANYTHIN—

THE FIRST THING I NOTICED WHEN I GOT THERE WAS THAT THE UNSEEN CLOCK HAD STOPPED TICKING.

THE SECOND THING WAS THE SMELL...

I CALLED MOM AND TOLD HER SOMETHING WAS WRONG WITH MR. WESTON.

HE WAS SORT OF SWINGING BACK AND FORTH BETWEEN ACTING "NICE BUT SAD"...

AND "MEAN AND LOST."

I COULDN'T HANDLE IT, SO I WAITED OUTSIDE FOR MOM.

WHAT DID YOU DO TO HIM?

WHAT CAN I SAY?

I KILLED HIS GARDEN.

WHY?

BECAUSE, HANA, NOW HE'LL NEVER ASK TO SEE YOU AGAIN.

IT'S WHAT YOU WANTED

I CALLED MOM AND SHE CALLED THE HOSPITAL...

AND THEY GOT TO MR. WESTON'S BEFORE HER.

HAS THIS MAN BEEN DIAGNOSED WITH ANY KIND OF NEURODEGENERATIVE DISEASE?

I... UHM... I DON'T REALLY KNOW HIM THAT WELL.

IT'S GONNA BE OKAY, SIR!

WHAT'RE YOU PEOPLE DOING IN MY HOUSE!!

CALM DOWN!

AVRIL?

AVRIL? I'M SORRY I'VE BEEN IGNORING YOU.

DON'T BE MAD. TALK TO ME. OKAY?

BEHIND YOU, SPORT.

AHH!

WOW, YOUR CLOTHES ARE... THEY'RE SO DIFFERENT IN THIS POSTER.

WE DON'T LOOK THE SAME ANYMORE.

YEAH, WELL... THINGS CHANGE.

WHAT DOES THAT MEAN?

IT'S NO BIG DEAL. I HAD THAT LOOK FOR A LONG TIME. SINCE I WAS A KID.

GUESS I'M JUST SORT OF... I DON'T KNOW, GROWING UP.

DO YOU THINK I LOOK STUPID?

CAR PAYMENTS

...SO THAT'S WHAT HAPPENED TO MR. WESTON.

IT SORTA PROVED TO ME THAT IT'S BETTER NOT TO CARE, YOU KNOW?

I MEAN, I HARDLY KNEW HIM, BUT STILL, IT HURTS SO BAD SO WHY GO THROUGH IT AT ALL?

HANA, HOW ARE YOU GOING TO GET RID OF THAT THING? THAT DEMON?

HE'S NOT A *DEMON*...

AND IT'S NOT HIS FAULT. HE WAS JUST DOING WHAT I WANTED.

THINGS ARE GOING TO BE BETTER REAL SOON.

I DON'T KNOW IF YOU'RE SEEING ALL OF THIS VERY CLEARLY.

WHAT DO YOU MEAN? YOU'RE NOT EVEN REAL. YOU'RE PROBABLY JUST MY FEAR TALKING.

BUT HE'S REAL, AND BECAUSE HE'S REAL THERE ARE CONSEQUENCES.

LOOK, HE PROMISED ME IT WAS GOING TO BE ALL RIGHT, OKAY?

HEAR THAT!? THE TRAIN'S COMING!

I LOVE YOU, HANA. BUT WHAT DOES MY LOVE MEAN IF I'M NOT REAL?

IF I'M JUST YOU PLAYING A GAME?

THE VISIT WITH AVRIL AND THE CUDDLY NIGHT'S SLEEP WITH MY LITTLE LIVING DOLL HAD HEALED ME SOME.

I MEAN, I STILL HAD A LOT OF GUILT ABOUT MR. WESTON.

OPEN ME!

BUT THERE WASN'T MUCH I COULD DO EXCEPT MAYBE USE MY LAST WISH TO MAKE IT RIGHT.

I'M OFF, MOM!

SEE YOU LATER, HON.

WHICH WAS SOMETHING I WAS CONSIDERING.

THING IS, THAT MORNING...

IT JUST FELT LIKE THINGS WERE ABOUT TO CHANGE FOR THE BETTER.

I WOULD BE LOVED.

# Get a sneak peek of *Make 5 Wishes*, volume 2 before it goes on sale!

Art by Camilla d'Errico

## Sign up for our monthly e-newsletter at www.delreymanga.com and we'll send you a link to special preview pages!

# ARTIST'S SKETCHBOOK
## Camilla d'Errico

## AVRIL

When I started to design the Avril character, I referenced a lot of her old pictures to see how she dressed. It occurred to me that Avril has a few different personas now, so drawing her as she was a few years ago at the height of her punk/rebel phase would have a different impact than if I was to draw her the way she looks now. I chose to picture Avril as she was early on because it made sense from a fan's perspective, especially Hana's, to want to idolize the rebellious Avril.

We all wish we could act out and
be free to express who we are. I
think that Avril really opens that
up for kids. In the story you
see that she does change. It was
important to deal with that issue
for Avril and for the story.

AVRIL CONCEPT
NUMBER ONE

Avril is always changing, as
are we all, so I wanted to
show her as she was and
as she is. Hana also goes
through a lot of growing
up, and that is reflected in
how we portray Avril (in
my opinion, anyway!).

## HANA

My dear little Hana! She has gone through quite a bit, actually. Her original name was Iku. I really liked that name, but we found out that it actually meant something quite unusual in Japanese, so we had to change it. Joshua came up with Hana, which is Japanese but still like a Western name.

I designed Hana to look like my younger sister. She has black, spiral hair that is quite long and really beautiful. As I started to draw her, she began to look a lot like I do. Hana's bangs, hair color, texture (my hair is also curly) . . . Suddenly someone who was supposed to be an homage to my sister became my twin. Personality was never an issue. She's a lot more like my sis than me—but we're sisters, so obviously we share some personality traits.

# ROMEO

My original demon was very evil. He/it spoke only to Hana and no one else could see it, so it was with her constantly, whispering in her ear to keep her from talking to others and basically reinforcing Hana's insecurities. The demon in this story is cute and cuddly! He isn't evil; he just thinks differently than we do. Since he isn't human, why should he think like a human?

I always loved Mark Twain's story "The Mysterious Stranger." In a way, Romeo is a lot like Satan in that context. All that cute stuff is Joshua—I had nothing to do with it, that's all Joshua! And why shouldn't our demon enjoy himself? He is a wishing demon, after all.

# ABOUT THE CREATORS

## ABOUT AVRIL

**AVRIL LAVIGNE** was born in the small town of Napanee, Ontario, Canada, and stood out from the crowd at an early age. Her musical talents were noticeable by the age of two, and by the time she was in her early teens she was already writing songs and playing guitar. Singing in the church choir and local festivals allowed Lavigne to get her voice heard.

On a trip to New York at age 16, Lavigne was signed to Arista Records when she caught the attention of Antonio "LA" Reid. With her major label deal signed, Lavigne moved to New York City, but not long after moved on to Los Angeles to work on her record. By early 2002, her debut CD, *Let Go*, was released. With 15 million albums sold, 8 Grammy nominates, and three #1 singles—"Sk8ter Boi," "Complicated," and "I'm With You"—Lavigne gave young women a defiant voice.

In 2004, Lavigne returned with *Under My Skin*. This time the Canadian chanteuse took charge of her creative direction and reflected a more introspective Avril. The album debuted at No. 1 on charts worldwide and delivered her fourth #1 single, "My Happy Ending."

Twenty-six million albums later, and following numerous awards, multiple world tours, and myriad magazine covers and TV appearances, Lavigne is now finding time to concentrate on her other loves, acting and fashion. Her third CD, *The Best Damn Thing*, releases in the spring of 2007.

# ABOUT THE ARTIST

**CAMILLA D'ERRICO** is an artist whose first love is the manga form. Her work will be featured by the underwear and lingerie company Ginch Gonch in their AIDS Awareness promotion scheduled for Fall 2007. In addition to the *Make 5 Wishes* series, she will have three comics published in 2007: *Burn*, a traditional manga series published by Arcana Studios in Canada; *Zevon-7*, a four-part miniseries published by AngelGate Press; and *Nightmares and Fairytales*, by Slave Labour Graphics.

# ABOUT THE WRITER

**JOSHUA DYSART** has been writing comics and graphic novels for a decade. He's been published by DC, Vertigo, Dark Horse, Image Comics, IDW, and many more and translated into four languages. His work includes two years on the legendary *Swamp Thing*; the adaptation of *Crouching Tiger, Hidden Dragon*; *Van Helsing Beneath the Rue Morgue*, an original story featuring the character from the Universal film; *Monster House: A Skull and Bones Story* from Sony's animated kids' feature; and *Age of Conan*, a comic to be included in the forthcoming massive multiplayer online game package. He's currently working on the epic miniseries *Conan and the Midnight God* at Dark Horse.

# AVRIL LAVIGNE

## THE NEW ALBUM
## the best damn thing

# AVAILABLE EVERYWHERE APRIL 17, 2007!

VISIT AVRIL'S OFFICIAL WEBSITE:
## www.AvrilLavigne.com

KILL YOUR DEMONS:
## Make5Wishes.com

GET THE HOTTEST OFFICIAL AVRIL GEAR HERE:
## www.AvrilMerch.com

JOIN AVRIL'S OFFICIAL MYSPACE PAGE:
## www.MySpace.com/AvrilLavigne